ALPHA HUNTER

An M/M Alpha/Omega Mpreg Novella

COYOTE STARR

Alpha Hunter

Copyright © 2017 by Coyote Starr

Published by BGE Publishing

ISBN: 9781521504147

All rights reserved under the International and Pan-American Copyright Conventions. No part of this book may be reproduced or transmitted in any form or by any means, electronic or mechanical, including phoocopying, recording, or by any information storage and retrieval system, without permission in writing from the publisher.

This is a work of fiction. Names, places, characters and incidents are either the product of the author's imagination or are used fictitiously, and any resemblance to any actual persons, living or dead, organizations, events or locales is entirely coincidental.

Warning: the unauthorized reproduction or distribution of this copyrighted work is illegal. Criminal copyright infringement, including infringement without monetary gain, is investigated by the FBI and is punishable by up to 5 years in prison and a fine of $250,000.

About Alpha Hunter
An M/M Mpreg Novella

Kill the monsters.

Don't fall in love with them.

And definitely don't have their babies.

Ethan spent his whole life training to hunt down and eliminate the deviant, all-male wolf-shifter packs—the ones made up of the Alphas whose ability to magically impregnate other males threatens the very fabric of shifter society.

Then an encounter with one man changes everything—especially when Ethan finds himself pregnant. If Ethan is himself a fertile Omega, then Jamal isn't really a fiend, and everything Ethan believes might be wrong.

And the more time Ethan spends with Jamal, the more he's beginning to think that maybe this baby is meant to be.

Assuming they can live long enough for Ethan to give birth—and to bring about peace among the shifter packs.

Love the Alphas.
Protect the Omegas.
Save the babies.

Book 1 of the hot new
Alpha Hunter Series!

DEDICATION

This novella is dedicated to Harper B. Cole, with love and thanks!

CHAPTER 1

The monster he hunted was so close that Ethan could hear the thing breathing. He couldn't pinpoint the sound's origin, though. The tombstones in this old cemetery redirected the noises and made the harsh rasping seem to come from every direction, even to his wolf-shifter hearing.

It might have been better if he could have shifted to his wolf form, but that made it easier for the deviants to track him.

No. Better to hunt them in his human shape, using human weapons.

Even if he couldn't hear as well.

He could hear Adrian's voice in his mind, the old Hunter scolding him in his rough voice. *Then do not use your ears.*

Ethan's sight wasn't of any use here, either. It was too dark—the gravestones and monuments, with their cracked and crumbling angel statues, were merely dark patches against a barely lighter sky.

Resting one fist lightly on the ground, he knelt behind the medium-sized mausoleum he had ducked behind when he first caught the breathing. He closed his eyes and let his senses fall away, one by one, focusing on each briefly to make sure he didn't need it.

Sight. Gone. Only the blackness of his inner eyelids.

Touch. He readjusted his grip on his broadsword, felt the grit of the dirt beneath the knuckles of his other hand, the pressure of the ground against one knee. Then he let his awareness of those things drift out of his consciousness.

Hearing. The other wolf's breathing sounded less harsh. It was catching its breath. Ethan had to hurry, or he wouldn't be able to catch it.

No. This can't be rushed.

Taking a deep breath of his own, he moved aside any idea of rushing, and simply allowed the sounds to slip away from his thoughts.

Taste. There was something there, a hint of an odd, wild flavor on the back of his throat. The taste of a rogue Alpha.

That sense he allowed himself to linger on, even as he moved to the last one.

Smell. With the shift in his focus to the scents in the air, that suggestion of something wild on his tongue became the full-blown aroma of the feral, the untamed.

The virile.

The monstrous.

And I know right where you are.

Opening his eyes, he allowed all his senses to flood back in, and this time, they all pointed in the same direction.

In one flowing motion, he stood and swung his broadsword in a smooth, silent circle, working out any kinks that might have developed during his sensory exercise.

As if he had become a shadow, Ethan slipped toward the nightmare slinking through the graveyard, coming on it from behind before it realized he was there.

This one was particularly ugly, caught halfway between animal and human form, standing upright on bent hind-legs, its wolf's muzzle highlighted in the moonlight as it turned its nose up into the air.

It caught his scent at the last instant, spinning around to face him as his broadsword whistled through the air, its centuries-old blade slicing cleanly through the flesh and crunching into the vertebrae. With a practiced move, Ethan jumped backward and tugged the broadsword out of the werewolf's neck to remove himself from the reach of its claws. It wasn't unusual for the creatures to swipe at him reflexively before their bodies realized they were dead.

Ethan had the scars to prove it.

But as long as he avoided a wolf's jaws, he was usually okay taking one of them out.

This one's body seemed to recognize that it was done for, though. Even as its mouth continued to snarl, its legs crumpled beneath it. Ethan watched dispassionately as it fell to the ground, attempting to determine whether or not he should step closer to deliver a final blow, or simply stand back as its last breath bubbled out.

When it dug its front claws into the dirt and attempted to drag its way toward him, he slipped to one side, dancing around behind it long enough to slam his broadsword down one more time. The head still wasn't entirely severed—it took much more precision and power to behead a monster in one stroke than most popular fiction suggested—but the creature fell still.

Once it stopped moving, he took the time to finish the decapitation. It never hurt to be certain, after all. Then he pulled a phone out of his back pocket. Nothing fancy—he didn't want to risk his good electronics on a hunt—but enough to let Adrian's clean-up team know where the body was. Adrian himself had been in Virginia scouting a new group, last Ethan had heard. But the old Hunter had promised Ethan he'd hit the road to South Carolina as soon as possible.

The lead clean-up guy would be glad to hear Ethan had finished this hunt in a cemetery. They were Adrian's favorite places for him to complete a kill, as they made body disposal much easier.

Planting the point of his broadsword into the ground and sliding his hand down the hilt, he squatted to get a closer look at the abomination's body, trying to determine if he could see any difference between it and his own packmates.

Alpha.

Yeah, right.

These creatures were not Alphas. Not in the way Ethan had been raised to believe.

They weren't leaders. Didn't have a pack.

Just the horrific ability to impregnate other men, the ones they called "Omegas." Sometimes, one of them went rogue and attacked a normal lupine shapeshifter, some poor gay pack member whose one-night-stand turned into a nightmare.

How must that feel? he wondered. To wake up from a night of passion, only to discover the most basic tenets of biology overturned...

To create life, another voice whispered deep inside him.

Not for long, though. Those poor males had their unnatural pregnancies terminated. Every once in a while, a pregnant male went crazy and tried to leave his birth-pack to join his attacker.

Those wolves had to be put down.

The thought of it made him sick. Shaking his head, he went back to examining the corpse.

Its mouth still held a sneer. The wolf had been in his late twenties or so, with a normal face and a half-beard that would not have suggested his deviant nature. The cloudy, sightless eyes had been blue, and at best, his physique could have been called rangy.

No. He was definitely not like any Alpha werewolf Ethan had ever seen. Just another clear indication that those mutants were abominations.

Sighing, Ethan pushed himself back up to standing.

Where the hell are Adrian's guys?

All Ethan wanted was a drink, and then bed.

Maybe someone else's bed, for a change. He rolled his shoulders. He could definitely do with the tension-relief a night of sheer, uncomplicated physicality could offer him— the kind of release he could get from sex, rather than killing.

Unless his clean-up crew bothered to show up pretty soon, though, the clubs would close before he had a chance to find someone to go home with.

There was a college campus not far away, he remembered.

Should be plenty of bars with lots of athletic, eager young men to choose from.

Even if talking to them did make Ethan feel unspeakably old, despite being only twenty-one himself.

Maybe he'd shift, go for a run first.

No. Definitely sex first.

At the sight of Adrian and his team making their way through the cemetery, Ethan raised a hand in greeting. As soon as he handed off this duty, he could start the real fun.

Time to get my game face on.

* * *

Jamal Akua leaned his elbows back against the bar and surveyed the crowded room. He hadn't wanted to come out tonight—college bars weren't really his scene, after all—but the rest of the pack had insisted, and as the only Enforcer who had traveled to the Summit with them, he felt it was his job to keep an eye on them.

"It is not your duty, son," Kamau, the pack leader, had told him. "Not tonight. We are here in peace. The other shifters will not attack." As he had left with the others, he had patted him gently on the arm. "If the summit does not go well tomorrow, we will be spending all our time looking for a new pack to trade Omegas with. That will be enough stress. Please, at least attempt to have a good time tonight."

So far, so good, really. Although alcohol didn't do much to burn through a shapeshifter's metabolism, five stiff drinks in a row had relaxed him enough that he didn't feel the need to glance over his shoulder every few seconds.

Relax.

The other pack Alphas were enjoying themselves, along with a couple of pack Omegas. And more than one or two of the humans in the bar had attached themselves to pack members, too. Jamal hoped the Alphas had remembered to bring condoms. The chances of interbreeding with humans were lower than they were with other shifters, but every so often it happened. A shifter baby born to an unsuspecting human parent was inevitably a problem. And if the unsuspecting human was male?

As an Enforcer, I would have to take care of that problem.

One way or another.

The pack leader wanted all wolf shifters—Alphas, Omegas, and even Betas—brought up within the pack. The Council wanted all shifters to remain hidden from general human knowledge. Everyone wanted the Omegas and babies protected. That meant it was a good idea to prevent unwanted pregnancies.

Jamal never wanted to have to kill a child's parent, if he could avoid it. He had been taught to revere fatherhood—even to removing a child from its father was more than he liked to consider.

A reminder to the Alpha males about protection won't go amiss, he decided.

He pushed away from the bar and stood up straight, moving lithely through the crowd toward Kopano. Leaning in toward the other man, he whispered a few words into his ear. Kopano's grin flashed wide and white, and he patted the pocket of his jeans with a wink. Jamal nodded, scanning the room for his next target.

A flare of golden-white hair caught his eye by the door, and he found himself staring at the blond man taking his ID back from the bouncer on the stool and gliding into the room.

He was far from the only white man in the place. Unlike other places Jamal had been in the Deep South, this bar's clientele was racially mixed—a side-effect, he assumed, of the nearby college, as well as perhaps a less volatile racial divide than he had been led to expect. But he was certainly the palest person, by far. Hair so light that only its gleaming gold highlights made it clear that he wasn't albino and milk-white skin both almost glowed, even in the bar's dim lighting. He carried a black leather jacket too warm for the weather, and his serious expression seemed to evaluate everyone in the room.

Jamal stood frozen to the spot, unable to look away.

The man's assessing stare slid past him, paused, and then tracked back until their gazes met. The stranger's eyes matched the rest of him—a blue so pale that they appeared almost colorless, except for a dark ring around the outside of the iris.

Like a wolf's eyes.

The thought shook Jamal out of his frozen state.

Could he be a wolf?

He needed to get closer, see if he could scent the male. At the thought of getting near enough to smell him, Jamal's breath caught in his chest, his cock stirring.

Getting next to the stranger had nothing to do with desire, he told himself.

If the blond was a wolf, Jamal he needed to let Kamau know.

And if he isn't a wolf?

Then Jamal needed to know that for himself.

Surreptitiously, he slipped his hand into his own pants pocket, glad to be able to double-check that he, too, had brought protection. He almost hadn't, sure as he had been that he would spend the evening watching over his packmates, rather than participating in the evening's sexual hunt.

You're still not certain that won't be your fate, Akua.

He was, nonetheless, glad to be prepared.

CHAPTER 2

After his initial survey of the bar, Ethan had paused, re-examining the composition of the crowd.

More wolf-shifters than humans.

More men than women.

More gay men than straight, it looked like.

That could definitely work in my favor.

Mixed-race group—but a disproportionate number of the men seemed somehow related, or at least linked. At first glance, he couldn't have articulated why, exactly, he had come to that conclusion. That they were all young, fit, black males who made similar fashion choices—mostly jeans and plain T-shirts—wasn't enough for that assumption. A bar in a college town was enough explanation for those similarities.

Closer scrutiny suggested that he was right, though. That particular set of men primarily spoke to one another, or to people they were hitting on.

Or to the one particularly muscular man who was making his way across the room, touching base with every one of the guys Ethan had pegged as being connected to one another. He watched him lean in to whisper to another man—instructions, from the way the other man nodded understanding.

Alpha male.

The thought flitted through his mind as his gaze flicked back to his face and they made eye contact.

At the impact of the man's stare, Ethan's breath hitched in his chest.

Damn, he's hot.

The muscular man slid around the edges of the bar, stopping to speak to several other men along the way, but always moving toward Ethan, his liquid-brown eyes flickering toward him every thirty seconds or so.

Yeah, he was every bit as interested in Ethan as Ethan was in him.

Smiling to himself, Ethan sidled up to the bar and ordered a drink. Something cold and strong was definitely in order. Even a cold shower after the hunt hadn't entirely cured his sense of being permanently bathed in a slight sheen of sweat. Charleston, South Carolina was not the sort of place he would want to have to live—or hunt—permanently.

Lucky for him, settling down wasn't an option—in Charleston or anywhere else.

We go where the monsters are.

I prefer it that way.

That's what he told himself, anyway.

He took a long sip of the drink the bartender handed him, letting the icy fizz of the tonic rest on the back of his tongue long enough for the bite of the gin to kick in, and then closed his eyes and sighed in appreciation.

"What are you having? Would I like it so much?"

Ethan opened his eyes and smiled, unsurprised to see the owner of the voice was the man who had been stalking him around the room. His voice was low and deep, his accent almost musical.

Tilting his head back, he regarded the dark man in front of him, who stood about two inches too close for someone Ethan didn't know. Close enough to be flirtatious, not so near as to make a lone wolf anxious. His dark brown eyes absorbed the light, reflecting nothing but liquid color back at Ethan. A dimple flashed in only one cheek when he grinned. "Well? Do you plan to tell me?"

Tilting his head to one side, Ethan glanced up at him from under his lashes. The man didn't tower over him. Oddly, he had expected him to—something about the guy made him seem bigger than he actually was, up close. "Gin and tonic," he said. "Nothing special."

"Not special? I do not believe it. All that you touch must become special." A half step closer allowed him to lean one elbow on the bar. Muscles in his arm bunched and flowed along his arm and up under the sleeve of his gray T-shirt. Ethan had to stop himself from reaching out to slide one finger along the smooth skin of his bicep.

At the mere thought of touching him, heat pooled low in his belly and his cock twitched in response.

Oh, yes. This one would do nicely.

Waving one finger in a lazy circle to encompass all the man's associates in the room, he asked, "You guys on some sort of team?"

That single dimple flashed again. "Something like that."

"I like your accent. Where are you from?"

"Most of us are originally from Botswana, in Africa, though many of us live here in the United States now."

"Soccer?" Taking another long sip through the straw, he assessed the man's responses.

"You mean football?"

With a shrug, Ethan let the glass clink to the bar and hooked a barstool with one ankle to pull it closer. Hitching himself up onto it, he leaned forward and, letting his voice go throaty, asked, "Does it matter what we call it, as long as we agree on the rules?"

"No. I do not think it matters at all." Finally, the other man stepped fully into Ethan's personal space, closing the distance between them.

* * *

Jamal pulled up short of actually touching the beautiful man in front of him, though the blond had all but invited him to do so every time Jamal looked at him. Jamal had immediately established that the other man was a standard Beta-male wolf shifter--unable to either give an Omega a child or bear one--but Jamal inhaled his scent a second time, just to be sure. The individual smell of a lightly scented soap, something like rain on fresh-turned earth, and clean sweat over pure man ignited a heat inside him like nothing else he had experienced before.

I should at least learn his name.

Even if every inch of him strained toward the blond, urging Jamal to clasp the man to him now. His cock had hardened instantly at the way the blond dropped his voice when he mentioned playing by the rules. From the way he leaned toward Jamal now, he felt the same way.

What Jamal wanted to do was shift his hand enough to bring out his claws and shred the boy's clothes until they were no longer in his way. Then he would lean the boy back, push his legs up high, and drive into him with every ounce of power he had.

He wanted to lose himself in the Beta.

But he knew better.

Betas couldn't take an Alpha's full strength—he'd tear the boy apart.

Jamal stifled a groan at the thought.

No. He would maintain control, even if everything about him called out to him to let go of his carefully cultivated restraint. Drawing in yet another deep breath, this one designed to help hold back his inner beast, he gently curled one white-blond lock of hair around his index finger. "What are you called?"

"Ethan." His voice came out in a rasp.

The artificial light of the bar glinted off the golden highlights wrapped around his fingertip. He trailed his other hand down the side of boy's face, watching the play of light on the dark skin of his hand contrasted against the golden glint of a slight beard.

The artificial light of the bar glinted off the golden highlights wrapped around his fingertip. "Such a dark name for someone so fair." He trailed his other hand down the side of his face, watching the play of light on the dark skin of his hand contrasted against his pale, soft cheek. He tilted his head to give him access to his neck, as well.

"And yours?" his wolf-bright eyes regarded him through half-closed lids.

"Jamal."

"Know what it means?"

Jamal nodded. "Beautiful, handsome—something like that."

Ethan smiled. "Sounds ... about right." The pause between his words drew out for a long moment as he looked around the bar.

"Want another drink?" Jamal asked.

With a slow smile and a long look that surveyed every inch of Jamal's body, Ethan said, "I think we could come up with a better activity for the rest of the evening."

With that, he placed his hands on either side of Jamal's face and pulled him down. As their lips met with an almost electric spark, Jamal felt his inner wolf chuckle with a happiness he didn't often feel—the two sides of his personality, beast and man, for once in perfect accord.

* * *

That first kiss in the bar had been almost intoxicating, even without the drinks. Ethan had intended to dive into the beautiful black man, to taste every part of Jamal that he could reach within the first few seconds. But the instant their mouths had touched it had been like everything around him slowed down. He could feel the warmth of his lips pressing against the other man's, the coolness of the air rushing into his mouth as he drew in a breath, the gentle pressure of Jamal's tongue flicking against the seam of his lips, urging Ethan to open his mouth.

That pressure became more demanding within seconds, and when Ethan's lips relaxed against his, Jamal's tongue all but dove into his mouth, their bodies pressing together. Ethan had never considered soccer a sport to particularly build one's upper-body strength, but Jamal's arms banded around him more intensely than he had anticipated, wrapping Ethan to him like silk-covered iron. Jamal's chest, too, pressed against Ethan with a pressure and a force he hadn't anticipated—but he welcomed it.

It had been a long time since Ethan had found anyone who could match him in bed; most of the men he picked up after a hunt were either humans—inherently too soft—or other wolves unwilling to engage in the kinds of sex-games that allowed them to play rough.

And invariably, the ones who wanted to play the kinds of games he did wanted to take it too far—they wanted to believe that they could control Ethan.

That would never happen.

All too often, the Hunter ended up hurting the man he picked up, either inadvertently or because he needed to put him back in his place.

With this man, though, Ethan suspected he might have found a match. Pressing his entire body against Jamal's, he pulled his mouth away enough to say against those amazing, full lips, "Do you have somewhere we can go?"

"Oh, yes, I do," Jamal rasped out in that sing-song accent of his.

"Then let's get out of here."

* * *

Outside, the air was thick and warm—autumn in the Deep South didn't cool things down much.

For once, Ethan was glad of it.

"Is your place nearby?" Ethan murmured into Jamal's ear, flicking his tongue along the shell of it in between words.

Jamal nodded. "Just a couple of blocks," he replied, pointing toward the hotel district, only a few blocks away.

Moments later, Ethan let out a low whistle as they entered the lobby of the Hyatt. "College soccer must be more lucrative than I thought," he said, raising an eyebrow as he glanced at Jamal.

Adrian would have told Ethan to hold his tongue, to practice fitting in with those around him. "A Hunter," he was fond of saying, "is all but invisible, in the world but not of it."

Tonight, though, Ethan was not a Hunter—or, if he was ("be always vigilant," Adrian would have scolded), he was a Hunter without a mission, at least for one evening.

Without a killing mission, anyway, he corrected himself. He definitely had a mission—and it was to get this hot man up to his room as soon as possible.

Ethan's companion didn't seem to mind him gawking at the hotel lobby. He simply laughed, and wrapped one arm around Ethan's waist to tug him toward the elevators.

Apparently, he had a mission, too.

In the elevator, Jamal pressed Ethan against the cool metal of the back wall, grasping his hands and sliding them up the wall behind Ethan. Jamal's kiss was deep and hard, and Ethan could feel every inch of the man pushing against him.

When the elevator doors opened behind them, Jamal pulled away only reluctantly, and led them down the hall.

When the door opened, Jamal threw both the key and the wallet onto the nearest flat surface and beelined for the bed.

Once there, Ethan stopped and ran his hand down the length of Jamal's cock, hard underneath his jeans. The contact sent a tremor through both men, and Ethan could feel himself harden even more.

Jamal pushed against his chest, backing Ethan up until the bed bumped against the underside of his knees.

Time to see if he really can keep up.

Jamal gave another shove—not hard, but not exactly gentle, either—and he sat down on the edge of the bed.

"Good boy," he murmured. "Aren't you the obedient one?"

"You have no idea," Ethan said.

"Then maybe I should find out."

"Oh, yes." His voice grew gravelly with desire. "Please, please do."

CHAPTER 3

Ethan crossed his arms in front of his body, grasped the hem of his shirt, and pulled it up and over his head. Holding it out to one side, he gave it a slight flourish before he dropped it on the floor.

Inside his jeans, Jamal's cock, already hard, strained against his pants. He could feel droplets of moisture from the head seeping into the fabric as he watched this beautiful, commanding man strip for him.

All too often, he had found, Betas were too soft for him. They wanted him to take charge, but were not willing to match his intensity. Worse, they were not willing to tell him what they wanted. He was not weak, but he was an Alpha wolf-shifter, and Omegas controlled their families and their clans. Omegas were not soft. He knew some wolf Alphas who had taken Beta playmates—even life-mates, though they were unable to have children together—but he had always thought there must be something wrong with those Alphas. He had never truly seen the appeal of it.

Until now.

This man, with his demanding mouth and determined hands—Jamal could imagine taking him for more than a night's playmate.

Slow down, Jamal, he reminded himself. See how the rest of the night goes, first.

The long, pale length of Ethan's body was almost all muscle, rippling as he reached down to untie his heavy boots and step out of them.

Everything about this man shouted strength and power. He moved with poise and confidence. And as Ethan stalked toward him in his bare feet and underwear, Jamal throbbed with desire.

Tilting his head back to stare up the length of him as Ethan came to stand over him, Jamal's breath caught in the back of his throat as the other man stopped only inches from him. Jamal could feel the heat rolling off his body, smell his desire, musky and raw, as the scent of it swirled around him.

He chuckled for the sheer joy of having found Ethan tonight.

"Something funny?" Ethan asked, tilting his head as he regarded him with those almost-white eyes.

"I am only happy," he replied, his smile still holding steady on his face.

"Touch me," Ethan commanded, smiling in return.

Jamal gently placed one forefinger on his chest. Then he drew it down, passing his waist and his bellybutton, and stopping at the top of his underwear, where Ethan's cock strained against the fabric.

"Like that?" he asked, a slight smile crooking the corner of his mouth.

Ethan didn't answer him directly, but instead issued another order as he stepped back. "Take off your clothes."

Without breaking eye contact, Jamal drew his shirt up over his head and dropped it on the floor, mimicking the gesture Ethan had made when he dropped his. He kicked off his shoes, shoving them under the bed. Then he unbuttoned his jeans, sliding the pants and boxers down his legs in one motion.

Ethan stood and watched all this without changing expression, still with that evaluative look in his eyes. His regard only made Jamal harder.

When Jamal stood naked, cock jutting out proudly, Ethan tilted his head to one side, his gaze sliding up and down Jamal's entire body. A slight breeze from the air conditioner drew chill bumps up on his arms. His inner wolf wanted to whine and yip with his anxiety for the blond's approval, but he shoved that desire down, focusing on the way Ethan's gaze narrowed when he saw Jamal's cock jump at the inspection.

"Oh, you like this," he said, the tip of his pink tongue flicking out against the corner of his mouth, and Jamal's breath left him in a rush.

Taking a step forward, Ethan pressed against the center of Jamal's chest with his palm, and then kept pushing him backward until Jamal first sat down, and then lay flat against the bed. Ethan crawled onto the mattress, placing first one knee and then the other on either side of Jamal.

Taking Jamal's hands in his own, Ethan slid their arms out to the sides, and then used his knees to press Ethan's biceps into the bedding, effectively pinning him to the bed by kneeling on top of him, his fabric-covered cock inches from his face.

With his dick this close, the scent of him surrounded Jamal, making him ache to wrap his lips around the blond. Jamal was strong enough to lift Ethan up, roll him under Jamal, and he could tell from the glint in Ethan's eye that he knew it, too, but he liked this game they were playing.

With the slightest lift of his head, Jamal could just barely touch his tongue to the fabric cradling Ethan's balls.

"Oh, not yet." Ethan's voice was throaty with desire, but he sat back on Jamal's chest, pulling the one part of him Jamal most wanted to lick farther away. Jamal's frustrated groan made Ethan bare his teeth in a smile, and Jamal moaned in complaint.

His breathing grew thick and heavy as he fought to lie perfectly still, waiting for Ethan to tell him what to do next.

"So, pretty boy," Ethan said. "What do you want?"

Jamal almost answered, "Whatever you do," but he could sense that wasn't the right answer. "To taste you," he finally said.

Fire blazed deep in Ethan's eyes, and with one hand, he tugged at his underwear sharply. They gave with a tearing sound, and he tossed the ruined fabric aside. Sliding forward, he pressed his knees into the mattress beside Jamal's ears, guiding his cock into Jamal's mouth.

With a deep sound of satisfaction, Jamal opened his jaws wide to suck, using newly freed hands to grab Ethan's ass and pull him down even more deeply into him.

* * *

The vibration of Jamal's moan against him made Ethan even harder than before.

Never had he met anyone who seemed to read exactly what he wanted as clearly as this man did. Nor had he ever found anyone so instantly ready to play the power games he enjoyed in bed. He wondered if Jamal would be able to switch roles as easily.

Maybe Ethan would try to find out.

Later.

Right now, he planned to slide his cock between Jamal's pliant pink lips, then push it as deep as he could, as hard and as fast as he could, until he came.

And oh, fuck, Jamal knew how to use that mouth, too, first sucking in the length of Ethan, then pulling away, and then—at just the right moment—opening wide enough to take it deep down his throat, wrapping his arms around Ethan's thighs to pull him down even farther.

At some point, Ethan realized, he had lost control of this game. Instead of directing Jamal, he was rocking back and forth, letting the other man pull him in completely and push him away again.

He might have been fucking Jamal's face, but Jamal was setting the pace.

Ethan's cock grew even harder and began throbbing as the pressure built inside him. Over and over again, Jamal brought him right up to the edge of release, and then backed off.

"Don't stop," Ethan ground out through gritted teeth, working to bury himself balls-deep in Jamal's mouth.

Jamal pulled away and bit Ethan's inner thigh just hard enough to make him gasp. "I want to fuck you," Jamal said. "And you're not ready yet."

"Make me cum first," Ethan demanded.

In a motion smoother than Ethan would have guessed possible, Jamal pushed him sideways. He would have tumbled to the bed next to him if Jamal hadn't flipped over and caught him.

Ethan was still catching his breath, and Jamal was already between his legs, his mouth nibbling and teasing Ethan's cock, sucking and pulling at it as he slid first one, then two fingers inside Ethan, using his thumb to trace heated circles along the underside of his balls as he rocked back and forth, faster and faster. With his other hand, he followed his mouth, slowing the pace once more but adding long, slow strokes, all but milking Ethan's cock into his mouth.

In only moments, Ethan felt the bright, hot point of his orgasm begin to build inside him, starting in his balls, then rolling through his abdomen. But again, Jamal stopped.

"Now you're ready," Jamal growled. Ethan could only moan in agreement. Whatever this man was planning to do, he was ready for it—but he still gasped in pleasure when Jamal pushed Ethan's legs high up against his shoulders, and buried himself to the hilt inside Ethan in one long, smooth motion.

Crying out in pleasure, Ethan met him, stroke for stroke, as Jamal pounded into him, and he whimpered when the black man slipped back out, wanting to clutch him closer.

But Jamal was far from done. He leaned back on his heels, rolling Ethan over and pulling him up onto his hands and knees. This time, when Jamal mounted him, pushing into him suddenly, in one motion, Ethan finally understood what it meant to be fucked by an Alpha, helpless in the throes of passion, desperate to cum but not allowed. Again and again, Jamal brought Ethan to the edge of release, only to bring him down again, until Ethan's cock ached with need.

With one hand, Jamal finally reached around Ethan's hip and wrapped his fingers around the other man's cock, caressing and fondling. Holding tightly onto Ethan, he began pulling him back, pushing deeper and deeper, slamming his cock into him from behind.

Again, Ethan met force with force, pushing back with his hands and knees to thump against him, grinding his ass backwards.

He had been right to choose this man, out of all the men in the bar. Hell, maybe out of all the men in the world.

Certainly out of all the men who had been in Ethan's bed, Jamal was the only one he had found who could match his intensity—both as giver and receiver of pleasure. Part of him wanted to draw this out longer, but even as Ethan's own orgasm began to build again, he could feel Jamal's dick inside him, growing harder and larger, filling him entirely as he got closer and closer to coming. Ethan could feel Jamal throbbing, and his fingers clutched the sheets under him as Jamal's balls slapped against his ass in a steady, harsh rhythm.

This time, when Jamal stopped him, it was to turn him back over. "I want to see your eyes when I cum inside you," he whispered.

Just the words nearly sent Ethan tumbling over the edge. And then Jamal was on him, in him—his cock filling Ethan entirely, even as he allowed most of his weight to rest against Ethan. The sweat-slicked skin of Jamal's abdomen, covered in a fine dusting of hair, rasped against Ethan's cock.

"Please," Ethan moaned, and this time, Jamal heeded the request, leaning in more and using one hand to hold Ethan's cock tight against his muscular stomach.

This time, Jamal didn't stop the building pressure, his own breathing harsh as he stepped up the pace. His liquid brown eyes seemed to glow with an inner light.

Ethan couldn't look away, drawn into those eyes, suspended in a moment of heated passion that he almost hoped might never end.

When Jamal came, it was with a hoarse cry and a pulsating heat that swelled inside Ethan, setting off his own orgasm. His cock jerked, pulling cum from deep inside him, taking his breath away as it exploded from him, leaving him thrashing as Jamal kept him pinned to the bed with his hands, his cock, and that magical stare.

* * *

Ethan watched with half-hooded eyes, feeling some combination of utterly relaxed and completely turned on as Jamal disappeared into the bathroom for a moment. When he returned, it was with a glass of water for Ethan.

"Here," Jamal said in that lyrical accent. "You must be thirsty."

Ethan sat up and took it from him, and as Ethan drank, Jamal pulled down one side of the comforter they had never bothered to take off the bed, setting up the pillows and gesturing him to the spot in an oddly gentlemanly fashion. Ethan allowed himself to be tucked in, feeling languorous and calm.

Tomorrow, he would have to go back to his real life, hunting and killing monsters, but just for tonight, he could revel in being well-fucked and treated nicely afterward.

Exactly what I was looking for.

When Jamal crawled under the covers on the other side and pulled Ethan against him, the Hunter didn't protest, though he usually didn't stick around for post-coital snuggling after a one-night stand.

This guy is different, he acknowledged.

For one thing, Jamal was just about perfect in bed, as far as Ethan was concerned—able to play rough, but gentle afterward.

It wouldn't make any difference in the long-term—Ethan was still a Hunter, would still be leaving before dawn—but for just a little while, he could at least pretend that there was more to this than a night of hot fucking.

"Talk to me," he said, tucking his ass up against Jamal's groin and his back against the other man's broad chest, reveling in the heat that poured off of him.

"Okay." Jamal's voice rumbled in his chest. "What shall I talk about?"

"You said you're from Botswana?" Ethan felt the nod as much as he heard the noise of affirmation. "Tell me what it's like."

Although Ethan had traveled all over the United States, and had even been to Mexico and Canada a couple of times, he'd never traveled to another continent. And unless one of the other Hunters needed him, he probably never would see any other countries.

Jamal began describing his homeland, the village he had come from, the people he had known there, and Ethan drifted off to images of the night sky, full of bright stars, over the plains of Africa.

CHAPTER 4

The buzz of Ethan's phone woke him for the second time the next day, sometime after noon, and he blinked away the sleep still fogging his thoughts and vision.

He glanced at the screen long enough to determine who had messaged him.

Adrian. Of course.

At least he was in his own, much shabbier, motel room. He had tiptoed out of Jamal's hotel room sometime in the wee hours of the morning, gathering his clothes and slipping into them, but carrying his boots in one hand until he reached the elevator. He had still been lacing them up as he hopped out into the lobby, and the single bellhop on duty had raised one eyebrow at him.

Fuck him, anyway, he had thought. It was none of his business what he was doing there.

That was what came of staying at fancy hotels with people who did things like carry luggage.

He had stalked through the streets back to his car, still in the parking lot at the bar. By the time he punched the key to open the door, his hair was damp with gathering dew.

Sleeping with that slight dampness to his hair, on top of the sweat-soaked sex before, must have messed with him—he felt slightly sick to his stomach.

No time for that now. Swallowing convulsively, he quickly scrolled through the messages to the latest one.

Rumor: Deviant pack meeting tonight. Call me.

So much for luxuriating in the sense of relaxation he had gained last night. Hell, he could already feel it dissipating as he instinctively began tensing up in preparation for a battle. His stomach continued to roil.

Battle with a whole pack, though? As far as he knew, Ethan was the only active Hunter in Charleston. Taking on a pack by himself wasn't wise.

No, unless Adrian had made arrangements with another Hunter to head this direction, his best bet would be to watch and wait, take out a few of the monsters at a time until he had thinned them down a little.

It would mean staying in South Carolina longer than he had intended to.

But it's not like I have anywhere else special to be.

Idly, he wondered how long Jamal's team was going to be in town. Maybe he could go watch them play.

Even better, maybe Jamal could let Ethan play with him again.

He shivered a little in remembered reaction. Damn, that had been amazing.

Deal with the abominations first, Ethan.

Setting a pot of coffee on to brew, he took a deep breath and prepared to speak to the elder Hunter, the man who had trained him, been his mentor—the man who had taught him everything he knew about hunting monsters.

The man who was about to quiz him about his activities the night before.

The activities he couldn't quit thinking about.

Ethan needed to get his mind on his job and off of the memory of Jamal's hands holding his ass, pressing into him and shuddering as he came.

It's none of Adrian's business, he reminded himself. He could just keep wondering.

He opened up the phone app, poured himself a cup of coffee, and prepared to dial.

But then one sip of the coffee—black, just the way he liked it—sent him running to the bathroom, heaving up bile.

What the hell? I didn't drink enough last night for a hangover.

Wiping his mouth, he took a careful sip of water, then brushed his teeth.

The roiling feeling didn't quite go away, but Ethan at least stopped feeling like he was about to boot again any second, so he carefully sat down on the edge of the mattress and tapped on his mentor's name in his phonebook.

* * *

When Jamal woke that morning, Ethan was gone. Somehow, he had known that would be the case, that their tryst the night before would not survive into the morning light.

He felt oddly disappointed, anyway.

But his list of things to do in order to prepare for that night's meeting with the South Carolina wolves would keep him too busy to worry about the beautiful, blond Beta with the bright eyes and an Omega's sense of play in the bedroom.

Right now, though, he needed to focus on making sure the South Carolina wolves didn't betray his pack. They were there to trade mating members—hopefully to diversify their genetic pool, if any of the pairs worked out. But the packs were wary of one another. And Kamau's pack was especially suspect, made up as it was of wolves of primarily African origin. Wolves who had left their homeland to make a different life for themselves.

Kamau might be certain the other pack would behave. Jamal was not.

His first step was to make sure that the square in the historic district where they would be holding their meeting was secure—or at least as secure as an open space in the middle of a commercial area of a major city could be. Still, the cities were the best places to meet. No wolf wanted to be caught by humans—but even more than that, they didn't want to share their own territories. Human cities were, by definition, neutral.

He knew Kamau would want to walk to the meeting site—he was already complaining of being cooped up inside too much on this trip—so Jamal chose to walk the short route between the hotel and the square. The morning air was cool and the walk gave him time to think.

Not that there weren't other dangers besides shapeshifters. Rumor had it that The Huntsman had been sweeping through the Deep South lately—the monstrous predator who stalked the Alpha and Omega packs across the world, using some sort of magical tracking skills.

Never mind the fact that most Alphas and Omegas avoided all-Beta packs at any cost. It was against Council law to kill a Beta—not out of any kind of morality, particularly, though Jamal saw no reason to harm beings that were, essentially, his biological siblings—but because the last thing the Alphas wanted was to confirm the Betas' worst fears: that they were not needed to perpetuate the wolf-shifters' lineage.

Beta packs outnumbered Alpha/Omega packs by ten to one, if not more. Their males mated with females. And their Huntsman killed any Alpha or Omega he found.

Different, not better or worse, Jamal thought, shaking his head in disgust.

Anyway, stories of The Huntsman were legion, and all depicted him as a giant of a man who carried a broadsword that could split an Alpha down the middle with one fell stroke, much as he had dispatched the werewolf who had made the mistake of attacking the very pregnant Omega Red Riding Hood and his witch of a grandmother. Despite being fairly certain that most of the stories were myth, Jamal felt equally certain that there was some kernel of truth to the legends—a person or group who tracked and murdered Alphas and Omegas.

If he was right, and there was a chance The Huntsman, or even some less-infamous huntsman, was nearby, Jamal needed to make sure he would find no way to pursue Kamau's pack.

The historic square was would do, he decided. It was surrounded by trees, but the vegetation was sparse enough that no human could conceal himself there. A child, or maybe a very small man, might be able to find a hiding spot. But not a huntsman.

* * *

Pulling on a dark hoodie over his jeans and black t-shirt, Ethan slid his dagger into its scabbard at his hip, slipped out of the nondescript car he drove, and moved into the night.

He raised the hood of the jacket over his bright hair, camouflaging it in the night. In his jeans pocket, he carried a compact filled with a black face-paint. If he got close enough, he'd smear some on to cover his pale skin. All his hunting clothes had been washed with baking soda and bagged before he packed them, and he had used scent-killing soap before dressing.

If he could have, he would've shifted into his wolf form. But he was less able to hide his scent in that form.

This way, he was as close to imperceptible to a shifter's heightened sense of smell as he could make himself. A handful of crushed leaves rubbed along his body would help cover what was left.

Adrian still favored the old ways—he kept a chunk of charcoal with him at all times. Ethan preferred a simple greasepaint.

But until he was actually ready to fade into the surrounding trees, he would actually draw less attention to himself if he avoided the wargames-style face-paint.

For a stroll through Charleston's historic district, a man in jeans and a hoodie was as unusual as he wanted to appear.

Of course, Ethan had been trained by Adrian, so he wasn't entirely unprepared, either. He had a few other tricks and even some stronger spells in his pockets—some flare-powder to use as a distraction if he needed it, a strength supplement, even a confusion spell. But spells too often went awry, and he didn't want to do anything to draw attention to himself in a city. They were neutral territory, after all.

He was still having difficulty believing that the deviant wolves were having a pack meeting in the middle of Charleston's most famous park in Marion Square.

As he moved down the sidewalk across the street from the square, he blinked at the figure of a dog that darted out from the underbrush and into a patch of darkness nearby.

Wait.

A dog?

No. A wolf.

Checking the air currents flowing around him, he moved around until he was downwind of the square before ducking behind a tree.

He caught a whiff of something similar to the scent he had gotten from the wolf he'd taken out the night before. Something wild and exotic. Something *other*.

Something laced with a trace of an almost-familiar fragrance that hadn't been there on the wolf the night before.

But whatever this new scent was, he had definitely smelled it before. Recently.

It had a pleasant association with it.

And then another wave of nausea hit him.

Ethan bit back a sound of annoyance as he swallowed convulsively.

Whatever was going on with him was fucking with his ability to tease out the constituent parts of scents.

I need to get closer.

Lowering his face to keep any moonlight from shining on it, he opened the compact and swiped his fingers through the paint, then dragged them across his face.

Ethan wasn't sure exactly how many monsters there were out there. He had taken down maybe a dozen in his time.

Ethan could barely make out several figures, man and wolf, milling around in the center of the square, and although he couldn't distinguish any specific words, he definitely heard voices.

The monsters would have set guards. That he hadn't seen or sensed any yet meant absolutely nothing. No matter, though. Far too many of them were milling about—he would never be able to take them all down.

He needed to get close enough to listen in, figure out what was going on. Then maybe he could track them back to their lair. Adrian was on his way to Charleston, already on the road. Working together, perhaps the two of them could figure out a way to take out a whole pack of the deviants.

Maybe two packs, given the clear lines of separation he was seeing.

I need to hear more.

Slowly, he shifted his weight forward, ducking down behind a line of ornamental bushes and working his way through the sparse underbrush centimeter by centimeter so as to avoid making any noise that might attract the wolves' attention. A single gap in the leaves caught his attention. If he could slide his eyes up to it without causing any of the foliage around him to rustle, he could watch the meeting— and maybe even hear what was going on, too.

Don't get too impatient, Ethan.

He could hear Adrian's voice. Be a shadow. Unseen. Dark. Unnoticed.

His own voice seemed to echo back mockingly. *Unvomiting.*

God. What was wrong with him?

Clenching his teeth against the sickness, he settled in to wait for his chance, moving only one muscle at a time, shifting in tiny increments until his face pressed up against the opening in leaves, his eyes gazing through the gap. The plants he crouched among had scratchy, waxy leaves that scraped against his face. Only years of training kept him perfectly still.

Well, training and the fact that he had finally gotten into position to both see and, mostly, hear what was going on.

Several wolves stood facing him in a semicircle, facing off across from a similar number of wolves. Behind them stood several men and women, the abominations in their human shapes, Ethan assumed. Some of the men were even visibly pregnant. Ethan sneered at the sight.

And at the center of the circle created by the creatures stood two men, engaged in intense conversation.

Whatever was going on here was something serious, and he could almost—*almost*—make out what the two people at the center of the circle were saying to one another in quiet voices.

But not quite.

Carefully, he slowed his breathing, letting most of his senses fall away, focusing on sight and hearing, waiting for the scene before him to come into sharp focus.

CHAPTER 5

Merely from the tense lines of Kamau's back, Jamal would have known that the summit with the other wolf pack was not going well, even if he had not been in the First Circle behind his lead Alpha, listening to every word.

"I was under the impression that your pack was here to engage in mating trade," Kamau said, his voice low and commanding.

"My pack does not need Alphas. We need Omegas. We do not need to give up any of our own Omegas."

"Every pack needs more Omegas," Kamau pointed out calmly. "We were assured both."

"I don't know who told you—" the Alpha began.

"The Alpha Council," Kamau interrupted. "Would you prefer to speak to them?" He waved a cell phone in the other Alpha's direction, and although he could not see it, Jamal knew that Kamau waited for an answer with one eyebrow raised, looking more patient than he probably felt.

"In any case," the lead Alpha continued, "if you are not here for a true mating trade, then we have nothing further to discuss." He began turning his back on the wolves.

That almost certainly had to be a bluff. Walking away from Alpha Council-coordinated negotiations could be a dangerous move.

"Wait," the other Alpha said, shaking his head. "What do you want?"

The tiny smile at the corner of Kamau's mouth disappeared by the time he was halfway around to facing the Alpha and his pack.

Ah. Now that the posturing is over, they can get down to the real negotiations.

Even in his animal form, it was all Jamal could do to keep from laughing aloud. He didn't even try to stop his tongue from lolling out to one side as he opened his mouth in a wolf-style grin. The wolf directly across from him hunkered down and snarled. Without turning around, the other pack's lead Alpha reached behind him with one hand and snapped at the growling animal, who instantly stilled.

Treats his people like dogs. Disgraceful.

Kamau would never do that.

Jamal allowed himself one more sniggering glance at the reprimanded wolf. Kamau might speak to him privately later, but he would never rebuke him in front of an opponent.

As Jamal raised his head proudly in the air, he caught a whiff of something ... familiar.

An image flashed across his mind of white-blond hair curling around his fingertips.

Ethan?

Here?

He sniffed again, but the scent was gone.

No. Wait. There it was again, like a bright, hot trail through the night air. He wanted to follow it, needed to, but as the only Enforcer here, he couldn't leave the First Circle during the negotiations.

But there was something else to that scent.

Something he knew well.

The scent of a gravid male—this one overlaid with Jamal's own scent.

What the hell?

Ethan was *pregnant*?

It wasn't unusual for an Omega to start showing signs of pregnancy this quickly. After all, a wolf in the wild had a gestation period of less than three months. It was no wonder that wolf shifters' pregnancies were shorter than humans' by several months. Add in the mystical element that allowed Omega pregnancies, and little about the timeline followed either a human or a wolf pregnancy.

No. What was unusual was that Jamal hadn't realized that Ethan was an Omega at all, much less a *fertile* one.

And he was absolutely sure that Ethan didn't know it, either.

Did the blond man even know what was happening to him?

I need to get to him. Protect him.

The almost irresistible urge to track his mate, keep him from any harm, rose up in Jamal.

Mate?

Oh, hell. I'm in trouble.

He could interrupt the summit, but doing so might ruin whatever finely tuned plans Kamau had in place.

What would he tell his lead Alpha, anyway? That he had scented the Beta he had brought back to the hotel the night before? Only he wasn't a Beta at all?

That I knocked up a Beta playmate who wasn't a Beta and now I know, all the way to my bones, that he's my life-mate?

Jamal was pretty sure Kamau planned to find a mate for him among the other pack's Omegas.

A string of blue curses flowed through Jamal's mind, but he managed to maintain an outward calm.

No. He would have to wait, see if he could follow the trail later, when the summit talks had ended.

And then one clear, unmuddled thought crossed his mind.

A baby. My mate is having a baby.

He needed to pay attention to the negotiations, in case they went awry. Kamau might need him to help keep the peace.

But that scent kept teasing his senses, drawing his attention away from the parley. Scenes from the night before unfurled before his eyes, and his beast all but laughed in delight. The wolf across from him curled a lip up to show a fang, assuming Jamal was laughing at him again. He wasn't—but he couldn't stop grinning, either, even though he knew that finding that scent here was not a good thing.

The way that muted smell kept teasing at him, drifting in and out of range, kept him half-distracted through most of the summit. He knew it for a pregnant Ethan's scent, but he couldn't pinpoint its location.

He did have a direction for it, though. At least, he thought he did. No matter how carefully he tilted his ears in that direction, though, he couldn't make out anything unusual, nothing beyond the general shifting and rustling that came with any large group of wolf-shifters, in any form.

By the time the leaders began wrapping up their discussion, it was all he could do not to go bounding off in the direction of the scent.

Kamau was summarizing the final agreement as it would be presented to the Alpha-Council, Jamal realized. It sounded like the Alphas were agreeing to an even exchange of Omegas. At the end of six months, any Omegas who hadn't mated would return to their home pack.

Excellent.

The need to mate was deeply encoded in both their culture and their biology.

Our animal sides control our actions more than we like to admit.

There were other elements to the agreement, but the trade was the one that Kamau had been most concerned about. It meant that his pack would have the chance to survive. To thrive.

Thank all that was good.

As the parley began to break up, Jamal couldn't help but aim a few *yips* at the wolf who had been snarling at him. The other wolves would recognize his voice, know that he was the one taunting their adversaries, but he didn't care. His mate was having a baby, and it made him feel like laughing.

* * *

Ethan had understood only about half of what the deviant wolves in the center were saying—something about trading Omega wolves?

In his own pack, Omegas were the least of the wolves, the last to eat in a group setting, the first to suffer taunts and gibes at the hands of their packmates. Among the deviants, they seemed to hold value as ... mate? Had he heard that right?

God. Were those the pregnant males? Was there something about them that made them more able to be impregnated?

The churning in his stomach reached new heights, and it was all he could do to keep from spewing on the ground.

At any rate, he'd heard enough to know that the deviants were planning to make a trade right here in Charleston in three days.

That would have to be his next move, then—take down the monsters during the trade. If he was right, if these Omegas were the ones who bore the babies, then eliminating them would eventually wipe out the whole pack.

Assuming Adrian agrees.

Sometimes, they butted heads over what direction Ethan's monster-hunting should take. Adrian was about half-likely to tell him not to take on one of the bigger packs.

But Ethan was good at hunting around the edges, taking down the stragglers, the outliers, then striking at the heart of the monsters—usually their leader. But in this case, their Omegas.

He just had to figure out who they were.

That would leave the packs in disarray, fighting among themselves.

And if I time it right, I can have them battling one another, as well.

He was certain that he was ready to take down a whole pack. He knew Adrian had done it more than once, back in his heyday, by combining with other Hunters.

Just because we prefer to work alone doesn't mean we're required to.

If there were two big packs of abomination wolves, then they needed to be put down.

As the discussion in the clearing began winding down, Ethan stepped silently backward, extricating himself from the foliage, moving carefully despite muscles that ached from remaining perfectly still for so long.

At the edge of the square, Ethan paused, still hidden by the leaves, to make sure no one saw him emerge from the vegetation. Covering up one hand with the sleeve of his hoodie, he swiped at the dark makeup on his face. As he prepared to step out onto the sidewalk, an odd yip stopped him.

Wolf, he realized. *I know that voice.* But whose was it? Something about it called out to him, as if pulling him back toward the clearing. *That's someone I know. I'm sure of it.*

He didn't have to leave. Technically, he didn't even need Adrian's approval to take out a pack. Having it helped, certainly, as he relied on the older Hunter for information and knowledge and even connections to his clean-up teams, half the time. But Ethan was a Hunter in his own right, trusted to make decisions in the field.

Instead of moving out of the foliage as he had originally planned, he turned around and made his way back to his viewing spot, where he crouched down and peered through the leaves again.

There. At the edge of the group, a white wolf looked back over its shoulder at its wolf counterpart from the other pack, its tongue lolling in an open-mouth grin, right before it let out another familiar, unnerving, barking laugh.

One of the men who had been involved in the negotiations fell back from his place in the middle of the group and put one hand on the wolf's back. It was enough to act as some sort of reprimand, or maybe just a reminder, as the wolf faced forward again and began trotting next to him as the man strode back to join the rest of the moving pack—but not without licking his hand, first.

Ethan shivered at the thought of the tongue on his own skin and had to shake off the response.

Tamping down his visceral reaction took a few additional moments. Any kind of emotional response could increase his scent and make him more easily detected by the deviants.

He felt compelled to follow that laughing wolf. Before he did so, though, he opened the package of baking soda he kept in the front pocket of his hoodie and sprinkled it over his hands, then patted it across his face, and inside his shirt. Finally, he dusted it across his hair and rubbed it into his scalp.

That should help keep him invisible, at least in terms of scent, as he followed the boisterous company.

The wolf-shifter pack didn't stay in a large group.

That was a smart move, Ethan had to acknowledge. The animals peeled off almost immediately after leaving the park, loping off into the darkness in ones and twos. Except the one he wanted. It stayed next to the man who led the group.

Soon, the men began splitting off, too—not a bad move, either. A large group of rowdy black men in the historic district of a city in the Deep South could look like a problem to some kinds of people.

If only they knew.

Race issues. Race was nothing. It didn't matter if people were black or white or goddamn *green*, as far as Ethan was concerned.

And any kind of wolf-shifter would have been fine with Ethan—as long as they reproduced in any normal kind of way.

He shook it off.

His goal was to put down one wolf shifter tonight, test their skills and strengths, and see if he could learn anything about them from it. Then he would make a plan to deal with the rest of them.

* * *

Jamal kept his senses focused on his surroundings, determined to protect Kamau and the other Alphas of the clan as they walked back to their hotel. When they turned onto King Street, he allowed Kamau to slide around him so that he walked on the building-side of the sidewalk, but only because sixteen-year-old Hawa walked on the other side of their lead Alpha, and he had aspirations of becoming an Enforcer himself.

Jamal had finally decided that Ethan must be gone—either that, or the scent he'd caught earlier was the product of wishful thinking—when a sudden gust of wind brought the smell to him again, this time clearly from somewhere behind them.

And just as clearly pregnant.

In the darkness, anyone who passed their group was likely to think him a dog, and although the thought of it galled him a little, he knew it was necessary to participate in the deception. At least stopping to sniff the air wouldn't seem particularly odd.

He couldn't help but revel in the scent of his mate.

After Kamau is safely returned to the hotel, he promised himself. Then he would go back out and track down the source of the scent that he found so distracting and alluring.

They were still several blocks from the hotel when Kamau stopped and pointed to a dark space between two houses. "Go. Change." He held out his hand to one of the Alphas, who pulled clothing out of a bag he carried and placed it over Kamau's outstretched arm. In turn, Kamau draped it across Jamal's back.

Jamal whined and pawed the ground, wanting to explain his need to track later and his desire to conserve the energy that an additional shift would expend, but his lead Alpha shook his head and pointed.

"Now. We will wait here."

Jamal didn't think Kamau would yield, even if he could explain.

Shifting this far from the land of his birth always hurt more than it had back in Africa. He couldn't explain it, or know why that should be so, but the other wolves had mentioned it, as well.

It left him feeling drained, as well, and ravenous.

Before he could go back out to track the elusive pregnant-Ethan-scent, he would need to eat.

And perhaps take additional food to his mate and unborn pup.

Even the thought made him grin again, even as his stomach growled.

From the sidewalk, Kamau laughed. "I heard that. Kopano just texted me. The other Alphas have gone to the hotel restaurant with the Omegas. You may join them."

Still buttoning his pants, Jamal stepped out onto the sidewalk, where he took a pair of leather sandals from Kamau and stepped into them. "After I see you safely back to your room," he said.

Kamau patted his cheek. "You are a good boy." Turning away, he headed back toward the river. "But the Betas are no threat tonight, and even if they were, I can take care of myself. We all can." With a wave of his hand, he encompassed all the Alphas surrounding him.

"But this is my job, and I will do it." Jamal knew he sounded petulant, but he had worked hard to gain the title of Enforcer, and he would not allow his lead Alpha to come to any harm—or even go out in public without a guard.

CHAPTER 6

Ethan slipped out of the shrubbery where he had hidden when the group had stopped, presumably for the wolf to change into its human form. He couldn't hear what they were saying or even see them clearly—they stood in shadows when they stopped, and moved swiftly and almost silently. But he could tell that the wolf had been replaced with a man.

Once, he had seen one of the deviants in the process of giving birth. The sight had horrified him—the man had dropped to his knees and twisted into impossible shapes as his body reconfigured itself to accommodate what never should have been—but it was the sound that stayed with him. Every time he thought of it, he remembered the grinding, crunching, cracking sound of bones and tendons popping.

If he'd had any sympathy for the beasts at all, it would have made his eyes water. As it was, his stomach turned whenever he considered it.

Tonight, with the odd churning in his belly, he couldn't help it—he finally gave into the urge and, as the wolves he tracked moved off, he leaned into the bushes and vomited.

I must have picked up something. Maybe from the guy last night?

It was weird, though—wolf-shifters were immune to most viruses.

No. He simply refused to allow himself to be sick.

With a snarl, he determined to follow this shifter group until he could either take one out tonight, or at least figure out how to do so soon.

The more they walked, the more he realized that he had been on this sidewalk before. Glancing up, he realized they were almost to the Hyatt. As the group ducked inside, he caught a glimpse of them in the light shining out through the glass doors from the lobby.

The man with them looked like Jamal.

He shook his head in an attempt to dispel the notion.

Ethan had killed dozens of deviants. He knew what they looked like, how they acted, how they smelled.

He knew how to recognize them.

He would never have sex with one.

By the time he reached the lobby door and stood just outside, peering in, the group was already halfway to the elevator. Scattered throughout the open area of the lobby, young black men stood in smaller groups, laughing and talking.

Oh, crap. He knew what this reminded him of.

The bar the night before.

The leader of the beasts glanced up, and his eyes caught the light, flashing it back toward Ethan in a glow that managed to be both yellow and brown.

As he pulled open the door, one of the men laughed. Another laugh answered it. That second laugh was bright and happy, and he had heard it before.

An involuntary gasp escaped him.

The beast really was Jamal.

He ran his gaze quickly over them, seeking him out.

Yes. There he was. Jamal was one of them.

"Oh, motherfucker," he breathed.

His stomach contracted and heaved again, as if he'd been sucker-punched.

Jesus mother-lovin' Christ.

I fucked one of the deviants.

His mind scrabbled away from the thought, instantly trying to find some way to justify it.

"Sir? May I help you?" One of the hotel's doormen leaned in to look at him from one side.

Crap. I'm blocking the entrance.

And worse than that, he was drawing attention to himself. Any second now, the monsters might take notice of him.

Jamal might notice him.

And he was going to need to stay hidden—to remain truly a shadow—if he was going to deal with this latest ...

Development? Event? Horror?

Fucking nightmare.

"No, thank you," he murmured, backing out of the door and letting it swing shut. He turned and walked purposely away, crossing the street to stand in the shadows cast by a tall tree.

He stared up at the hotel for a long moment, trying to gather his disordered thoughts. After a minute, he began pacing back and forth along the sidewalk across the street from the entrance, until he noticed the doorman watching him with too much interest.

"Dammit," he muttered, crossing the street again and cutting through what looked at first glance to be some kind of alleyway.

Ethan was half-tempted to turn around and present himself at Jamal's hotel room, demanding to know who and what he was.

That would give away his own identity as a Hunter, however.

But he wasn't going to follow his original plan of *take out a deviant to learn their strengths and weaknesses*, either.

No. He was going to take one of those monsters prisoner and make it talk. Force it to tell him everything it knew about their packs—their Alphas and Omegas—and why one would want to have sex with a man he couldn't impregnate.

Still fuming, he stomped back toward the hotel, grinding his teeth in combined anger and horror.

How dare he act like a ... a *person？ A regular wolf-shifter?*

And to think Ethan had actually liked the deviant.

Liked *him.*

Oh, dear God. I let it fuck me. Cum inside me.

Ethan's stomach clenched, and he doubled over, retching. By the time he stood up, wiping the back of his hand across his mouth, he felt calmer. More certain of himself.

I can't waste any more time on emotions.

I have a job to do.

Step one of that job was to re-acquire his target.

It had been a mistake to let the group he had been following out of his sight. Ethan was willing to forgive himself the lapse, as he had been taken by surprise and allowed his feelings to overwhelm him.

That wouldn't happen again.

I wish I had my broadsword with me, though. I could work through a lot of emotional angst with it.

Perhaps he would shift to his own wolf form, after all.

Closing his eyes, he let himself fall into the trance that allowed him to flow into his wolf form.

Nothing.

Frowning, he stared down at his still-human form. A frisson of fear shot through him.

What the hell?

He had barely enough time to finish the thought, when hard hands grabbed him from either side. Before he could overcome his surprise enough to shout, a dark SUV with tinted windows pulled up to the curb, and he was shoved into the back seat, followed by one of the men who had grabbed him.

Sitting in the seat next to him was another man, tall and still dark-haired despite his age, and on the floorboard, a wolf.

"Adrian?" Ethan asked, still stunned.

"What?" his mentor said as the driver in the front hit the gas. "Did you think we wouldn't smell that abomination all over you?"

Ethan simply stared, open-mouthed.

"We know you're pregnant with that deviant's devil-spawn."

* * *

Jamal waited until the door to Kamau's suite had closed behind him and the other Alphas of the clan, then turned and raced back to the elevator, all but bouncing on his toes.

He was absolutely certain that down in the lobby, he had seen a flash of white-blond hair out of the corner of his eye—someone leaving the lobby, though by the time he turned around, it was gone, and the elevator had arrived.

He didn't want to hope that Ethan had figured out he was pregnant and had come to tell Jamal, but he found himself considering the possibility, anyway.

And if he has, so what? a sarcastic inner voice asked him. *You will request that this man you just met be your mate for life?*

It was stupid, he knew that. Other than their sexual compatibility and the fact that they were going to have a baby together, Jamal had learned almost nothing about Ethan.

Then again, many successful relationships had been built on less.

I'm an idiot.

But a hopeful idiot, he thought as he dashed through the lobby and out the door, stopping at the sidewalk to gaze about in all directions.

And perhaps a disappointed one, as well. No flash of blond hair caught his attention. If it had actually been Ethan leaving earlier, Jamal had wasted too much time seeing Kamau to his room to be able to see him now.

Still, he sniffed the air, hoping to find a trace of him on the breeze.

Instead, he smelled something entirely different.

Wolf. One he didn't recognize, and nearby, too.

He had just enough time to spin around to check his surroundings, when a dark SUV pulled up in front of him and the door swung open.

Rough hands grabbed him from behind, moving shifter-fast. He had only begun to struggle against them when he was shoved roughly into the SUV's already-crowded back seat.

One that already held Ethan. Sitting next to another man who all but exuded Alpha pheromones.

Did I fuck a man who was working with the other pack?

Could Jamal's intuition about him have been that wrong?

Surely not.

Ethan looked as unhappy to be in the car as Jamal did, his jaw clenched tight as he stared down the wolf in the floorboard.

Then Jamal saw the gun the Alpha had jabbed in Ethan's ribs. He definitely wasn't here by choice.

Of course, Ethan's gaze wasn't any more pleasant when it flickered toward Jamal than it was when he glared at the Alpha-wolf.

Jamal held his silence until they pulled up in front of some sort of warehouse several miles from the hotel. The wolves ushered them out of the SUV at gunpoint, and took them into a large, empty room. There, Ethan and Jamal were both chained to chairs and the chains run through bolts cemented into the concrete floor.

They remained silent for a long moment after the wolves had left them alone in the room, and he continued to glare at him steadily.

Stonily.

"Are you okay?" Jamal finally ventured. "Did they hurt you?"

"Why didn't you tell me you're a goddamned deviant?" Ethan hissed at him.

Deviant?

The word ricocheted around Jamal's head until it made him dizzy with realization.

Oh, hell. Not only was Ethan not a Beta—he was from a het-pack, one of the ones that procreated heterosexually.

He didn't know he was an Omega.

He probably has no idea that he's pregnant, even.

Or maybe he did.

"What do you know?" Jamal asked, his voice more tentative than he had intended.

"I'm an Enforcer," Ethan replied stiffly. "And I know that since I was a child, it's been my sacred duty to remove the deviants from wolf-kind, to eliminate the abominations. To make the wolf-packs great again."

Wait. What?

"Oh, holy shit," Jamal breathed out. "You're The Huntsman."

"I'm a Hunter. The Huntsman is a myth—but yes, it's based on us."

"But you're a shifter."

Ethan stared at him, confused. "I'm both. I'm a shifter and a Hunter. Isn't that why you chose me? Isn't that why you turned me into a deviant, put this abomination into my belly?"

"No. Ethan, no." Jamal found himself leaning toward his mate, straining against the chains. "I had no idea you were a Hunter. I didn't even know you were an Omega. Much less that you were fertile."

"Then why?"

"I was drawn to you. I still am. I want to protect you, protect our baby."

"Did you know I can't even shift?" Ethan demanded. "I tried, and I couldn't change into my wolf form."

Jamal nodded. "It's standard with Omegas, to help them avoid hurting the baby. It's why Omegas *need* Alphas to protect them."

Tears welled up in Ethan's eyes, and Jamal had to choke back his own.

They were still staring at each other when the werewolves who'd kidnapped them returned to the room.

"So," said the Alpha. "The monster and his whore. Together. Glad we'll be able to take you both out at once."

Another werewolf in human form opened the door a crack and slipped into the room. "I found the Huntsm—the deviant's car," he said. "Right where you said it would be."

He tossed the keys to the Alpha.

Ethan glanced from the Alpha to Jamal and back again, and then, without warning, began to laugh.

"You have no idea," Ethan said. "You taught me everything you know, Adrian, and yet the instant you think I'm one of them, you act like I can't fight back."

Ethan's glance invited Jamal to join in the joke, though he wasn't entirely certain why. It seemed to disconcert the Alpha—apparently Ethan's Huntsman trainer, Adrian—so he added his own cackle to Ethan's wild laughter.

Then the chains securing him to the chair and to the floor exploded, and everything around them went to hell.

CHAPTER 7

Ethan wished he'd had a way to warn Jamal of what was about to happen. But the werewolf gave him the idea when he'd called Ethan a whore.

Apparently he can't think of me as both a baby-maker and a Hunter?

He curbed the thought, with a glance at Jamal. Despite his emotional reaction earlier, and even to the news of his own pregnancy, Ethan found himself still attracted to Jamal, physically. And his very first words had been to make sure he was okay.

I'm so fucked.

So to speak.

Because for the first time ever, Ethan understood why the Omegas fought so hard to protect their cubs.

With Jamal next to him, the scent of him drawing Ethan in, he *wanted* this baby.

He could feel the beginning flutterings of life in his belly.

This wasn't an abomination.

This was a miracle.

And he wanted to make sure this baby had every opportunity to thrive in the world.

Not that his change of heart mattered, if they couldn't get away. He had no doubt that Adrian's team would kill them both. He had seen it in their eyes and was a little surprised that they hadn't already done so. Clearly they wanted something from either him or Jamal.

In the meantime, they seemed to be waiting for something.

Ethan decided to take advantage of that wait, wiggling around until he got one hand into his back pocket.

If Adrian hadn't slipped into thinking of Ethan as one of them, he would've been sure to check Ethan's pockets and disarm him.

For the first time ever, Ethan thanked Adrian silently for having trained him to pack along back-up supplies rather than relying on his shifter abilities.

With a flick of his wrist, he scattered flare-powder in front of himself, closing his eyes as it exploded. Then he followed it with the confusion spell, holding his breath and counting to ten to let it take effect on the others while he ripped the bolts up out of the floor, first the one holding his chains down, then the one holding Jamal's—the chains were strong, but he had already seen that the bolts were rusted, and his natural shifter strength, combined with his strength as a Hunter was easily equal to the task. Next, he smashed the chairs, once again breathing normally, but counting silently.

At most, he had thirty seconds to get them out before the confusion spell began to wear off and Adrian's team figured out what was going on.

Thirty seconds to get to his car and either get them both out of there, or grab his broadsword—along with all the other supplies he kept in his trunk—and take a stand.

He would decide which when the time came.

"Come on."

He grabbed Jamal's hand and tugged, but Jamal resisted, as confused by the spell as the other wolves were.

"Shit. I don't have time for this." He placed his palms on either side of his face, stared into his eyes. "Jamal. It's me. Ethan. From last night. Remember? I'm..." he paused before forging ahead. "I'm having your baby, and I need you to come with me."

He didn't know what he would do if Jamal refused—if the other man fought back, Ethan wasn't sure he'd be able to pick him up and carry him.

Leave him behind?

And suddenly he discovered that he was absolutely unwilling to do that.

I am really and truly fucked.

Luckily, Jamal nodded and fell in behind him.

Ethan heard him muttering one phrase over and over as he followed him out the door: "Our baby. Our baby. Our baby."

Ethan ignored his mutterings and pulled out his last spell packet. This one he sprinkled into his mouth, grimacing at the taste, then waited for the strength-enhancer to kick in.

When it flooded his system, he took the length of chain still wrapped around his hands and focused on pulling open one link, then another. When he was free, he slipped the chain through the handles and managed to bend it back on itself just as Adrian and the wolves on the other side began slamming into the door.

Only then did he look back at Jamal, who had used the time to shift into his wolf form. He still dragged chains from around his midsection, but up close, his animal shape was huge, reaching almost to Ethan's waist, and heavy-boned. The white fur looked soft and thick, and Ethan had to fight the urge to bury his hands in it.

He's beautiful.

There was no time for that now, though.

He reached out his hands to pry the chains away from Jamal's midsection, and as the chains dropped to the ground, found himself rubbing his fingers through the gorgeous fur—it was every bit as soft as he'd imagined.

"Later," he promised, though whether to himself or Jamal, he wasn't certain. All he knew for sure was that the hinges on the doors were about to give, and he still didn't have his weapon.

Scrabbling toward the car, he managed to open the driver's door and pop the trunk, and by the time the doors fell outward from the frame to reveal three full-grown wolves, he and Jamal stood side by side, ready to fight.

* * *

They fought, Jamal thought, as if they had been built to work together. Ethan moved like a dancer, his broadsword flashing bright in the moonlight.

Jamal, used to hunting with his packmates, darted in and out, snapping at the wolves and using his sharp teeth to slash skin and heavy jaws to crush bones when he caught them. The first wolf he grabbed yelped once as Jamal cracked his foreleg in half, then went silent forever as Ethan cleaved through its spine with his weapon.

Dropping the dead wolf's leg, Jamal turned to guard Ethan as he pulled the broadsword's blade from the animal's neck.

But the other wolves were leaving, turning to trot away into the night, Adrian clearly willing to let the two of them go rather than risk his own skin. But as Adrian backed away, too, he called out, "This isn't over, *deviant*. We're coming to get you."

Jamal snarled at their retreating forms.

Ethan tilted his head as he watched them go. "Not if I can help it," he whispered. He dropped one hand to Jamal's head. The other slipped to his abdomen, caressing it unconsciously. "I think maybe we had better get out of here, find someplace safe to call your people from."

Jamal yipped in agreement, and Ethan seemed to understand.

"Yeah," he said. "Let's go."

He paused long enough to grab the clothing Jamal had stripped out of before shifting only moments ago. "I assume you'll need these when you change back? And that you *can* change back sometime soon so we can talk?

Jamal yipped again, twice this time, and Ethan nodded, then opened the back door for the enormous wolf. Then Ethan hopped in, setting his broadsword in the floorboard of the passenger side in front.

They drove for a long, silent time. Ethan had no idea where in Charleston they were, but he didn't really care.

Everything about his world was about to change.

He was going to have to reevaluate everything he thought he knew.

As soon as he felt certain no one was following them, Ethan pulled the car off onto a side street, then wound through as many turns as he could bring himself to make, just to be sure, before pulling over to the side of street and switching off the car.

Turning sideways, he stared for a long moment at the man—in human shape again, for now, and dressed in jeans, if nothing else—in the back seat of his car. Finally, he asked the first question that came to mind.

"How?"

Jamal narrowed his eyes, considering what to say—or maybe how to say it. "Omegas didn't come out of nowhere," he finally said. "We used to all be the same pack. We're...different branches of the same evolutionary tree. And sometimes an Omega is still born among your packs."

Ethan bit his bottom lip, worrying at it. "Will your people accept me?"

Jamal laughed out loud, the bright sound making Ethan smile in response. When he answered, though, it was in a soft tone. "They will love you. And our baby."

After a long moment, Ethan joined Jamal in his joyful laughter, then leaned over the seat to pull him into a deep, hot kiss.

There would be more questions later, he was sure—many more, and some hard choices to make. But Ethan was certain that Jamal was right: if they stayed together and worked to protect their child, they could navigate what was to come.

They might not know what this was, or where it was going, but Ethan was absolutely certain he was going to enjoy the ride.

"Our baby," he agreed, murmuring it against Jamal's lips.

* * *

Six months later

"Oh, God," Ethan groaned, clutching his stomach. "All the wolves I've killed. All those Omegas and their babies." Bending over the edge of the bed, he vomited into the bag the doula held for him, heaving until there was nothing left in his stomach.

"You didn't know," Jamal tried to soothe him for about the millionth time. "You believed what you were told."

"Is Adrian still hunting the Omegas? We didn't catch him yet?" They'd moved Ethan out of sight for the duration of his pregnancy, though he'd been involved in the new resistance against the Hunters by providing information about the men who tracked his new pack and their kind.

"Not yet." Jamal kept his voice low. "But we will. You don't have to worry about that now, though."

The next contraction rippled across Ethan's stomach and his face scrunched in a pain that took so much concentration that he couldn't even scream. Sweat dripped from his face.

"This better be fucking worth it," he gasped, glaring at Jamal, after the contraction passed.

"It will be. I promise," Jamal said, leaning in to brush the hair off his lifemate's forehead.

"It's time to move to the birthing chair," the doula said, his voice calm and soothing, as it had been through the entire fourteen hours of labor.

Jamal nodded, slipping his arm behind Ethan's back and helping him lean forward. Ethan paused, gripping Jamal's shoulder. "Look at me. Jamal. If something happens to me—"

"Nothing's going to happen to you," Jamal interrupted. "Everything's going to be fine."

"Listen." He stopped, rocking with the pain of another contraction. When it passed, he gasped out, "If something happens to me, you must protect our baby. Keep him safe from the Hunters."

Jamal nodded, his face serious now. "I will," he vowed.

"Good. Now get me to that chair."

Hours later, Ethan lay exhausted in their bed, Jamal next to him, baby Andre nestled in between them.

Looks like I was able to settle down, after all.

As he watched Jamal kiss the top of Andre's head, Ethan finally understood, in a way he hadn't until now—all that mattered was love. And this family he and Jamal had created was pure love. Not Alpha, not Omega, not Beta.

Just love.

Perfect love.

And he would fight—forever, if necessary—to protect that love.

* * *

Love this book? Be sure to leave a review!

Keep an eye out for the next Alpha Hunters book!

Love the Alphas.
Protect the Omegas.
Save the babies.

About the Author

Coyote Starr is the pseudonym of a *New York Times* bestselling author whose love of M/M stories couldn't be contained by just one pen-name.

Printed in Great Britain
by Amazon